This book belongs to

_____

Published by Advance Publishers
© 1998 Disney Enterprises, Inc.
All rights reserved. Printed in the United States.
No part of this book may be reproduced or copied in any form
without the written permission of the copyright owner.

Written by Lisa Ann Marsoli
Illustrated by Stacia Martin and Yakovetic
Produced by Bumpy Slide Books

ISBN: 1-57973-010-8

10 9 8 7 6 5 4 3

The fairies Flora, Fauna, and Merryweather loved Princess Aurora. After all, they had raised her from the time she was a baby. Because of them, the evil Maleficent's spell had been broken. Now the Princess was safe and engaged to marry her true love, Prince Phillip. The fairies couldn't have been happier.

"It's going to be a beautiful wedding," Fauna sighed as the kindly fairies watched the young couple strolling in the castle gardens.

"Of course it is! We're going to make sure of that," Flora said.

"What do you mean?" asked Fauna.

"Well," Flora began, "we can't trust just anyone with the preparations for the wedding. We must see to it ourselves!"

"You're right," Merryweather agreed. "We must go to the King and Queen and ask that we be put in charge of every last detail!"

King Stefan and his queen agreed to the plan right away. They were grateful to the fairies for having saved their daughter's life.

"It would be an honor to have you take care of the wedding," the Queen said graciously.

That very afternoon, the fairies made a list of all that had to be done.

"Invitations need to made, addressed, and delivered," began Flora.

"And we'll have to create a beautiful bouquet for the bride to carry," added Fauna.

"And a spectacular cake," Merryweather continued.

"Don't forget the music, and Princess Aurora's gown," Flora reminded them.

On and on the fairies went, long into the night, scribbling down more items as they went.

The next day, the fairies rose early, ready to get to work.

"Let's begin with the invitations," Flora suggested.

Together the fairies went to the room in the castle that held shelves and shelves of fancy paper.

"I like this kind," said Fauna, holding up a sheet of creamy yellow.

"Oh, no, this is much better!" Flora replied, waving some pink paper with a scalloped edge.

"Wedding invitations should always be white," disagreed Merryweather. "I'm sure the Princess thinks so, too!"

"Dears," Fauna interrupted, "let's not bicker. There's plenty of time to settle on the invitations. Why don't we choose some flowers for the Princess's bouquet instead?"

The other fairies agreed, and soon they were in the garden surrounded by every kind of flower imaginable. Flora wanted the Princess to carry roses. "Just like the name we gave her — Briar Rose," she insisted.

But Merryweather said that roses were a bad idea — their stems were so prickly with thorns.

"There's plenty of time to decide," Merryweather said. "Why don't we go see about the wedding cake instead?"

In the kitchen, Flora, Fauna, and Merryweather leafed through a recipe book with the royal baker. Flora pointed to the picture of a three-layered cake. "What about that one?" she asked.

Merryweather shook her head. "That cake is much too small to feed the entire kingdom."

"I could make it bigger," the baker suggested.
"I think we should have lots of smaller cakes instead of a large one," Fauna said.
"Ladies," the baker said gently, "why don't you come back when you decide?"

Next the fairies were to meet Princess Aurora
at the royal dressmaker's. When Flora, Fauna, and
Merryweather arrived, the Princess greeted them
warmly. "Isn't this lovely?" she asked, holding out
a length of ivory-colored satin.

"It is pretty, dear," Flora agreed, "but what about this silk? See how beautiful it looks?" She circled Merryweather, covering her in fabric.

"What about this velvet?" Fauna said, also winding the cloth around Merryweather.

As Flora, Fauna, and the Princess discussed their choices, Merryweather toppled to the floor. "If no one minds," said Merryweather, freeing herself, "could we choose the fabric another day?"

The search for just the right music to play at the wedding went no better. Flora, Fauna, and Merryweather simply couldn't agree. After the royal musicians played song after song for the fairies, the court composer threw up his hands in despair.

The day before the wedding, Flora, Fauna, and Merryweather had a meeting to check on what still needed to be done. Their list of what remained read: invitations, flowers, food for the feast, the wedding cake, music, and Princess Aurora's gown.

"But . . . but . . . that's everything!" Flora said in horror.

"I wish we'd been able to make up our minds!" moaned Merryweather.

"I'll never forgive myself!" Fauna wailed. "We've ruined the Princess's wedding!"

"Wait!" cried Flora, her face brightening. "I have an idea!" With a flourish, she pulled her magic wand out of the folds of her dress. "There's still time to arrange a magnificent wedding."

"What a perfect plan!" agreed Fauna. Then she and Merryweather took out their magic wands, too.

"We're going to have to give our wands double the power to get so much done so quickly!" said Flora as she divided up the list of tasks. "Be back here in an hour. It will take *all* of our magic to make a wedding gown fit for the Princess."

And with that the fairies went scurrying off to their various tasks.

Merryweather went straight to the room that held the fancy paper, and waved her wand in the air. "Invitations make yourselves, then fly down from all your shelves!" she commanded. Within seconds, hundreds of pieces of paper folded themselves.

Next Merryweather aimed her wand at a nearby pen and inkwell. The pen scribbled words on the invitations and addressed the envelopes to all the guests. Then the invitations flew out the window, landing on doorsteps throughout the kingdom.

Meanwhile, Fauna attended to the wedding
cake. She went straight to the kitchen and asked
the royal baker to bring out the cake he had made
for that night's dessert.

Fauna concentrated on the simple cake before
her. When she waved her wand over it, she said,

"Magic wand, make this cake grand, so that it might feed all the land!" Immediately, the cake began to grow bigger and fancier, and it was soon almost as big as the table upon which it sat.

"Perfect!" thought Fauna as she scurried off to her next task.

Outside, Flora flew over the garden. She smiled at her wand and said, "Send your magic down below and make Aurora's bouquet grow!" Then she chuckled a satisfied chuckle. "By the time I return, the Princess will have the most beautiful flowers imaginable! But first, I'd better meet Merryweather and Fauna. I don't want them to make the wedding dress without me!"

Flora, Fauna, and Merryweather stood looking
at a simple dress from Princess Aurora's closet.
Soon it would be a magnificent wedding gown.

The fairies held their wands poised over the dress. Flora closed her eyes and began, "Make a gown for a lovely bride," and Fauna finished, "with a train so long and wide."

Then Merryweather added, "And since you are three wands, not one, we expect a job well done!"

A swirl of fairy dust surrounded the dress,
then disappeared. What stood before them was
an exquisite gown indeed, but its train was so long
it stretched across the floor, out the window — and
clear to the other side of the kingdom!

It was just then that Princess Aurora appeared carrying a bouquet of weeds. "I found these in the garden," she said. "What are they for?" Then she caught sight of the wedding gown. "And what happened to that dress?" she wondered.

Suddenly a loud CRASH was heard in another part of the castle. Moments later, the royal baker rushed in. "It's the cake!" he cried in alarm. "It's still growing — and it just broke through the roof!"

"Oh, Princess!" Fauna cried.

"We're sorry!" said Flora. "We couldn't agree on anything, so we had to use our wands to get everything ready for the wedding in time. We made them work so fast and so hard that their magic came out all wrong!"

Princess Aurora smiled sympathetically. "We could always postpone the wedding," she offered.

"No, we can't," said Merryweather. "The invitations have already been sent."

Princess Aurora just smiled and held up an invitation that had accidentally landed in the garden. All the letters on it were backwards!

"Well, we certainly made a mess of things,"
Merryweather admitted.

"But I think I know what to do!" Flora said.
Then she told the other two fairies her plan.

Soon the fairies were using their magic to
put everyone to sleep. Next they turned back
the calendars so that it was weeks before the
wedding. When they woke everyone up, no one
in the kingdom had any idea what had happened.

The fairies sat together, composing a list
of preparations for the wedding. On the first day,
they chose roses and violets for the Princess's
bouquet, decided on a recipe for the wedding cake,
and settled on the perfect song to play as Princess
Aurora walked down the aisle.

On the second day, they addressed the invitations. Then, when they were through, they began choosing the fabric and pattern for Aurora's gown.

On the third day, Princess Aurora stopped by with the King and Queen.

"Are we interrupting anything?" the Princess asked.

"No, no, please come in!" the fairies insisted. "We hope you'll be pleased with what we've done."

"So the preparations are going well, then?" asked the Queen.

Flora, Fauna, and Merryweather all looked at one another, trying hard not to giggle.

"Um . . . right on schedule, Your Majesty!" exclaimed Fauna.

"

There once were three good fairies
Who had a lot to do,
But they could not agree, and so
Their work was never through!
But if they'd made decisions
Together, as a team,
They never would have needed to
Cook up a magic scheme!